Living Lights™ A Faith Story

The Berenstain Bears®
Read-Along Classics

5- Minute Inspirational Stories

By Stan and Jan Berenstain
with Mike Berenstain

ZONDERKIDZ

The Berenstain Bears 5-Minute Inspirational Stories
Copyright © 2017 by Bearenstain Publishing, Inc.
Illustrations © 2017 Berenstain Publishing, Inc.

Requests for information should be addressed to:

Zonderkidz, 3900 Sparks Dr. SE, Grand Rapids, Michigan 49546

ISBN 978-0-310-76080-1 (hardcover)

The Berenstain Bears God Loves You! ISBN 9780310712503 (2008)
The Berenstain Bears Say Their Prayers ISBN 9780310712466 (2008)
The Berenstain Bears Love Their Neighbors ISBN 9780310712497 (2009)
The Berenstain Bears Faithful Friends ISBN 9780310712534 (2009)
The Berenstain Bears The Forgiving Tree ISBN 9780310720843 (2011)
The Berenstain Bears and the Biggest Brag ISBN 9780310734796 (2014)
The Berenstain Bears and the Gift of Courage ISBN 9780310712565 (2010)
The Berenstain Bears Blessed are the Peacemakers ISBN 9780310734819 (2014)
The Berenstain Bears Get Involved ISBN 9780310720904 (2012)
The Berenstain Bears' Gossip Gang ISBN 9780310720850 (2011)
The Berenstain Bears God Bless Our Home ISBN 9780310720898 (2012)
The Berenstain Bears Here's the Church, Here's the Steeple ISBN 9780310720812 (2011)

Design: Diane Mielke

Printed in China

17 18 19 20 21 22 23 24 25 /LPC/ 15 14 13 12 11 10 9 8 7 6 5 4 3 2 1

CONTENTS

The Berenstain Bears®
God Loves You!

The first week of school was a busy time for Brother and Sister Bear. It was a time to see old friends, meet new teachers, get their first homework assignments, and sign up for after-school activities.

Sister decided to try out for the big school show. This year it was *The Music Bear*. Sister thought she would be perfect in a leading role. She liked to sing "I Feel Pretty" from *Bearside Story* at home. Mama and Papa always said she was very good.

But there would be a lot of other girls trying out for the show too. Babs Bruno had a very fine voice, and there was Queenie McBear, of course. She thought she was the best singer in the school, and all her friends agreed with her.

HE
BEAR
JOUTS

er

Brother Bear was trying out too, but not for the school show. He wanted to be on the school basketball team. He was pretty sure he could make it. He had been practicing dribbling and layups in the driveway at home. He played 21 with Papa after supper and always beat him.

The tryouts for the school play and basketball team were on the same day. After school, Brother went down to the gym and got into a basketball uniform. He and the other boys charged out onto the court and started warming up.

Sister joined a long line of cubs in the auditorium. Teacher Jane called them up on the stage one by one to sing a song. Babs sang "Memory," and she was very good. But Queenie made a mess of "Tomorrow!" She had a hard time hitting all the high notes. In spite of that, all her friends clapped and cheered, and Queenie took a few bows. Sister glanced over at Teacher Jane. She didn't look too impressed.

When it was Sister's turn, she sang "I Feel Pretty" just like she did at home for Mama and Papa.

In the gym, Brother was trying hard to look good. Coach Grizzmeyer looked on and checked off names on a clipboard. You couldn't tell anything by watching him. His face never changed. The cubs called him Old Stoneface.

Finally, he said, "Okay, men! That's enough! The roster will be posted on the bulletin board outside my office tomorrow."

Brother couldn't resist stopping to ask, "Coach, do you think I have a shot at making the team?"

Coach Grizzmeyer just shrugged and said, "We'll see, son."

In the auditorium, the auditions for the school show were winding down. Teacher Jane smiled a lot more than Coach Grizzmeyer, but she wasn't giving anything away, either.

"That's all for today, everyone!" she said. "I'll post my choices for the entire cast tomorrow on the bulletin board outside my room."

As Sister left, she couldn't resist stopping to ask, "Teacher Jane, do you think I have a chance of getting one of the main parts?"

But Teacher Jane just smiled and said, "We'll see, my dear."

Sister joined up with Brother as he walked home from school.

"Well, how do you think it went?" asked Sister. "Do you think you made the team?"

"Yeah, I think so!" said Brother hopefully. "What about you?" Brother asked. "How did the auditions go?"

"Great, I think," said Sister.

"What did Teacher Jane think?" Brother asked.

"I don't know," said Sister thoughtfully. "She didn't say anything. She just smiled at everybody."

"At least she smiled. Old Stoneface never smiles!"

The next morning, both Brother and Sister rushed downstairs, gobbled their breakfasts, waved a quick good-bye to Mama and Papa, and got to school faster than they ever had before.

They couldn't wait to see how they had done. Brother rushed to Coach Grizzmeyer's office while Sister scurried to Teacher Jane's room. There were crowds of cubs gathered around the bulletin boards.

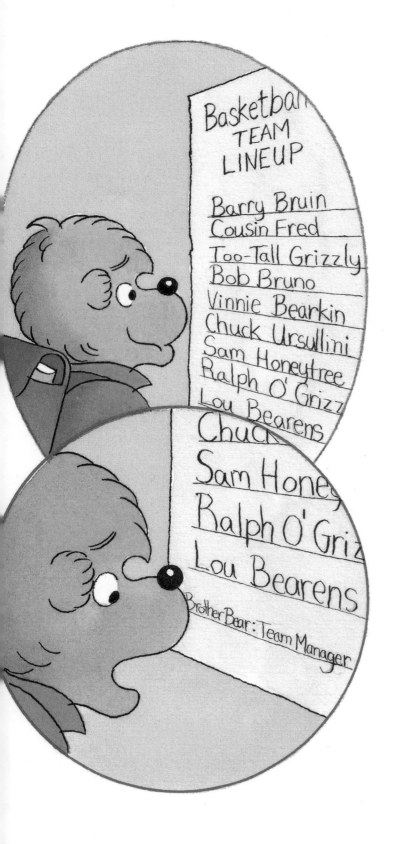

Basketball
TEAM
LINEUP

Barry Bruin
Cousin Fred
Too-Tall Grizzly
Bob Bruno
Vinnie Bearkin
Chuck Ursullini
Sam Honeytree
Ralph O'Grizz
Lou Bearens

Chuck
Sam Honey
Ralph O'Griz
Lou Bearens

Brother Bear: Team Manager

Brother glanced quickly down the list of names. There was his, right at the bottom. At first, he felt a rush of relief. But then, he noticed what it said next to his name: Team Manager.

Team manager! TEAM MANAGER? The team manager just picked up basketballs and made sure everybody got on the bus on time. That's not what he wanted to do! He wanted to play. He wanted to be a big star! Crushed, he slunk down the hallway to his classroom.

Outside Teacher Jane's room, Sister quickly looked over the cast. At first, she didn't see her name at all. Then she spotted it, right at the bottom. Sister Bear: Stage Manager.

Stage manager! STAGE MANAGER? All the stage manager did was put away the props and make sure everybody got onstage on time. She didn't want to be stage manager. She wanted to act. She wanted to be a big star!

Miserably, Sister trudged down the hall to her classroom.

When school let out that afternoon, Brother and Sister were both feeling very sorry for themselves.

"Whatever is the matter?" asked Mama when the cubs arrived home.

"Yes," said Papa. "You both look like you are about to get a tooth drilled."

Brother and Sister sighed.

"Oh, we had a rough day at school," said Brother. "I didn't make the school basketball team."

"And I didn't get a part in the school show," added Sister.

"How disappointing!" said Mama. "Didn't Coach Grizzmeyer or Teacher Jane give you anything to do at all?"

"Well," said Brother, "they did give us something to do. I'm the team manager."

"And I'm the stage manager," said Sister. "But I don't want to do that! I want to be in the show!"

"And I want to be on the team!" said Brother.

"Well," said Mama, "I guess not everybody can be a star."

"But don't you think I deserve to be in the show?" asked Sister.

"Of course you do!" said Mama, giving her a hug. "You're a wonderful singer!"

"And don't you think I deserve to be on the team?" asked Brother.

"Of course you do!" said Papa, patting him on the shoulder. "You're a terrific basketball player!"

"I guess nobody else thinks so," said Sister gloomily. "I guess nobody at Bear Country School thinks much of us at all!" She heaved an even bigger sigh.

"Well," said Mama, "it's not going to do us any good sitting around here feeling sorry for ourselves. Why don't we all go out for a little walk?"

"But it's raining," protested Brother.

"The rain's stopped," said Papa. Sure enough, the clouds had lifted and the sun was peeking out.

By now, the clouds had all rolled away and the golden sun was shining over the countryside.

"Look!" said Papa. "A rainbow!"

"Wow!" said Brother. "It's so bright!"

"What makes a rainbow?" asked Sister in wonder.

"Well," said Papa, "you see ... the light from the sun shines through the raindrops and creates a prismatic thingy, which bounces around from the um ... uh ..."

Mama interrupted. "The rainbow is a gift from God. It's a sign that the rain is past and the sun has come to warm the earth again. God puts the rainbow in the sky as a beautiful sign of his love for all the earth and all the creatures that he has made."

"Even us?" asked Brother.

"Of course!" said Papa. "God loves everybody!"

"Does he love us even when we're bad?" wondered Brother, a little puzzled.

"Well ..." said Papa.

"What about when we're really, really bad?" asked Sister. "Like when Brother and I got into a fight and wouldn't speak to each other for a week?"

"Um ..." said Papa.

"YES!" Mama broke in, suddenly. "He does!" They all looked at her in surprise.

"God wants us to be good but he doesn't love us because we're good or bad. God loves us because he made us. It's a little bit like how mothers and fathers love their children."

"Oh," said Sister. "Like how you still love us even when we do things we're not supposed to?"

"That's right," said Papa. "Of course, we're disappointed when you misbehave. But we still love you! We even love you when you don't make the basketball team or get a part in the school show! And we're proud of you because your coach and teacher trusted you to be managers—special jobs for the most responsible cubs."

Brother and Sister smiled. They were beginning to feel slightly better about that little problem.

By now they had made their way down the lane to a spot that overlooked Farmer Ben's farm. It was a lovely scene. The cows were coming in from the pasture, the ducks were swimming in the pond, bees were buzzing around their hives, and the sun was setting behind the trees.

As the sky grew darker, they noticed a tiny point of light in the western sky.

"What's that?" wondered Brother.

"That's the evening star," said Papa. "It comes out just after sunset."

"Is that another sign of God's love?" asked Sister.

"Yes, dear," said Mama, giving her a hug. "It surely is!" And, hand in hand, the Bear family turned for home and their evening meal.

The Berenstain Bears
Say Their Prayers

It was bedtime in the Bear family's tree house—bedtime after a long, busy day. Little Honey Bear was already asleep in her crib. Brother and Sister were ready for bed too. They were bathed and they had their pajamas on. Mama and Papa were done reading them their bedtime stories. But there was one last thing to do before they went to sleep. It was time for Brother and Sister to kneel down beside their bunk bed and say their prayers.

25

Tonight when Mama and Papa were giving the cubs their goodnight kisses, Brother asked a question. It was a question he had been thinking about for a while.

"Mama," he said. "Why do we say prayers before we go to sleep? I was at Barry Bruin's house for a sleepover last week, and he doesn't say prayers at all."

"Some people just don't believe in saying prayers," said Mama. "But we pray at night so we can thank God for the blessings of the day."

"Good night now," said Mama. "Sweet dreams."

"Hmmm …" thought Brother, as he drifted off in the sleepy darkness. Mama's answer was okay. But he still had a few questions.

The next morning, Brother and Sister were up early. It was Saturday, and they had a Little League game with their team, the Sharks.

"I feel hot today!" said Sister. "I feel a whole lot of hits and stolen bases coming on!"

"Oh, yeah?" snorted Brother. "What about home runs? I guess I'll have to take care of that department!"

"Sure!" said Sister. "Brother Bear, the Home-Run King!" She ran, laughing, out of the room with Brother Bear chasing her. Sister and Brother liked playing on the same team. But sometimes they got a little too competitive.

After breakfast, the whole family headed down to the ball field. Brother and Sister had practice before the game. It was Mama and Papa's turn to help with the snack bar. Papa soon had the grill behind the snack bar fired up. Mama opened up the candy stand, and Honey Bear started getting into the cotton candy.

The team ran out on the field.

Today, they were up against the Pumas. The Pumas were one of the best teams in the league. Their lead-off batter was a big, powerful cub twice Brother's size. He was twirling six bats around his head in the warm-up circle as if they were a bunch of twigs.

"Uh-oh!" said Brother. "Look who it is!" Sister gulped. It was the Beast—the Pumas' best player. He could hit and field and pitch. They didn't know his real name. They just called him the Beast.

Brother glanced over at Fred on the mound. He looked pretty nervous out there.

"Play ball!" called the ump, and the game was on.

The Beast picked out a bat from his bunch and stepped into the batter's box. He glared at Fred on the mound.

Brother noticed Fred wasn't glaring back. In fact, he was standing quite still, his head bowed and his hands folded. It looked like his eyes were closed, and his lips seemed to be moving.

"Psst, Fred!" called Brother. "What's up?"

But Fred didn't answer. He straightened up, took a deep breath, and went into his windup. He fired a fastball. There was a swish and a thump! The Beast had missed!

"Stee-rike one!" called the ump.

"Way to go, Freddy baby!" yelled Brother. "That's the way to pitch 'em in there! Just two more like that! You can do it!"

There was another swish! And another thump! "Stee-rike two!" yelled the ump. Another swish and a thump! "Stee-rike three!" called the ump. "Yer out!"

Fred didn't look nervous anymore. Now it was the batter's turn to look nervous. Fred threw six more fastballs to two more batters. There were six swishes and six thumps. Cousin Fred had struck out the side!

"That was some pitching, Fred," said Brother later on as they sat on the bench waiting to go up to bat.

"Thanks," said Fred.

But there was something else on Brother's mind. "I was wondering, Fred," began Brother. "What were you doing out there with your head down like that?"

"Oh," shrugged Fred, a little embarrassed. "I was just praying."

"Praying?" said Brother in surprise. "What were you praying for—strikeouts?" Before Fred could answer, it was his turn to bat. He trotted out of the dugout, leaving Brother still wondering.

By the end of the game the Sharks were in a tough spot. They were behind by one run with two outs and a man on base. The "man" was Sister. She had gotten to first on a walk and then stolen second—she was a feisty little player. Now it was Brother's turn to bat. If he could get a hit, the Sharks might tie it. If he got a home run, they would win.

The Pumas' pitcher was none other than the Beast. As he walked to the plate, Brother felt a little sick. Talk about pressure!

Before he stepped into the batter's box, Brother decided to do something he had never done in a baseball game. He bowed his head, closed his eyes, and said a prayer. "Dear Lord," he prayed. "Please let me get a hit."

Feeling a little more confident, Brother stepped up to the plate. The Beast wound up and let it fly.

"Stee-rike one!" called the ump.

Brother gripped the bat tighter. He'd get the next one. Another scorcher screamed past.

"Stee-rike two!" called the ump.

Brother clenched his teeth. The Beast wound up, the ball flew, and Brother swung—hard!

Swish! Thump! "Stee-rike three!" bawled the ump. "Yer out!"

The game was over. The Sharks had lost, and Brother had struck out!

"Way to go, Home-Run King!" shouted Sister in disgust. Brother trudged back to the dugout. He had never felt so awful in his life!

"Don't let it get to you," said Fred. "That was a tough game. The Pumas are a good team."

"Yeah," agreed Brother. "I tried everything. I even tried praying like you did when you struck out the Beast. But it didn't work for me."

"Really?" said Fred. "What did you pray for?"

"I prayed for a hit, naturally," said Brother.

"Oh," said Fred, rubbing his chin. "I see."

"Why?" asked Brother. "What did you pray for?"

"I just prayed that I wouldn't get too scared," said Fred simply.

Brother blinked at him. "I guess your prayer was answered!"

"Prayers are always answered," said Fred. "Sometimes, we just don't get the answer we expect."

That evening at bedtime, Brother and Sister knelt down beside their bunk bed to say their prayers. Tonight, they felt like a nice long one:

"Bless Mama, bless Papa, bless Honey Bear, bless Grizzly Gramps, bless Grizzly Gran, bless Cousin Fred, Uncle Willie, and Aunt Min. Bless our friends Lizzie and Barry, and bless Teacher Bob, and ..."

As Brother lay drowsily in his bed, he started thinking over the day's baseball game.

"That was a tough game today, wasn't it?" he said to Sister.

"Yeah," answered Sister. "Tough on you, Mr. Strike-Out King."

"What's that supposed to mean?" said Brother, glaring up at the bottom of her bunk. "I played my best! A strike out like that could happen to anybody!"

But Sister didn't answer. She was fast asleep. Brother rolled over and ground his teeth. Sometimes Sister Bear made him so angry he could just … But then he thought of another prayer.

"Dear God," he prayed. "Please help me with my little sister!" And to his surprise, he found his prayer had been answered. He didn't feel angry anymore.

"Thanks for the help up there!" he said. And with a sigh, he fell asleep.

The Bear family was quite proud of their handsome tree house home, and they worked hard to keep it neat and tidy. The trim was freshly painted, the front steps were scrubbed, and the windows were washed. The lawn was mown, and the flower beds were weeded. Even the leaves of the tree were carefully trimmed and clipped.

Most of their neighbors took good care of their homes as well. The Pandas across the street were even bigger neatniks than the Bears.

Farmer Ben's farm just down the road was always in apple-pie order too. Even his chicken coop was as neat as a pin. "A place for everything and everything in its place, that's my motto," said Farmer Ben.

The Bear family had a few neighbors whose houses were positively fancy—like Mayor Honeypot. His house was three stories tall and built of brick. It had a big brass knocker on the front door and statues of flamingos on the front lawn.

Even more impressive was the mansion of Squire Grizzly, the richest bear in all Bear Country. It stood on a hill surrounded by acres of gardens. Dozens of gardeners took care of the place.

The Bear family was proud of their neighborhood, and they got along well with all their neighbors.

Except for the Bogg brothers.

The Bogg brothers lived in a run-down old shack. Chickens, dogs, and cats ran everywhere. A big pig wallowed in the mud out back.

"Those Bogg brothers!" Mama would say whenever she saw them. "They're a disgrace to the neighborhood!"

"Yes," agreed Papa, "they certainly are a problem."

One morning, the Bear family was working outside, when the Bogg brothers came along. They were driving their broken-down old jalopy. It made a terrific clanking racket.

As they drove past, one of the Bogg brothers spit out of the car. It narrowly missed the Bears' mailbox.

"Really!" said Mama, shocked. "Those Bogg brothers are a disgrace!"

"I agree," said Papa. "I'm afraid they're not very good neighbors."

Papa looked through the mail and found a big yellow flier rolled up. He opened it and showed it to the rest of the family.

"Oh, boy!" said Sister and Brother. "It's like a big block party! Can we go?"

"It certainly sounds like fun," said Mama. "What do you think, Papa?"

"Everyone in town will be there," said Papa. "We ought to go too."

"Yea!" cried the cubs.

On Saturday morning, the Bear family all piled into the car. They were looking forward to a day of fun and excitement.

But, as they drove along, the car began to make a funny sound. It started out as a *Pocket-pocketa-pocketa!* But it soon developed into a *Pocketa-WHEEZE! Pocketa-WHEEZE!*

"Oh, dear!" said Mama. "What is that awful sound the car is making?"

Just then, the car made a much worse sound—CLUNK! It came to a sudden halt, and the radiator cap blew off.

They all climbed out, and Papa opened the hood. "I guess it's overheated," said Papa.

"Oh, no!" said Sister. "How are we going to get to the Bear Town Festival?"

"Maybe someone will stop and give us a hand," said Papa hopefully.

"Look, here comes a car. Let's all wave. Maybe they will stop."

It was Mayor and Mrs. Honeypot. They were on their way to the festival too. Their car slowed down, but it didn't stop. The Mayor leaned his head out of the window.

"Sorry, we can't stop!" he said. "We're late already. I'm Master of Ceremonies today. I've got to be there on time. I'm sure someone will stop to help you."

And he pulled away with a squeal of tires.

"Hmm!" said Papa. "Maybe someone else will come along."

Soon, another car did come along. It was Squire and Lady Grizzly being driven to the festival in their big black Grizz-Royce. They slowed down too. Lady Grizzly rolled down her window.

"I'm afraid we can't stop," she said. "We don't have time. I am the judge of the flower-arranging contest. We simply must hurry."

And with that, they pulled away.

"Maybe no one is going to stop," said Sister. "Maybe we're never going get to the festival."

"One of our neighbors is sure to stop and help us," said Mama. "After all, that's what neighbors are for."

"Yeah," said Brother. "But do they know that?"

A cloud of dust appeared down the road.

"Here comes
someone now!" Sister
said eagerly.

The dust cloud drew closer, and they could hear a
clackety racket getting louder.

"Uh-oh!" said Papa, shading his eyes and peering
down the road. "If that's who I think it is …"

It was!

It was the Bogg brothers.

They came clanking up in their rickety old jalopy and
screeched to a halt. First one, then another, then another
of the Bogg brothers came climbing out.

"Howdy!" said the first Bogg brother. "I'm Lem. I can see yer havin' some trouble with your ve-hicle."

"Well, yes, we are," said Papa.

"Maybe we can give you a hand," said Lem.

"That would be very neighborly of you," said Papa.

"Hey, Clem! Hey, Shem!" called Lem. "Git out the rope!"

The other Bogg brothers rooted around in the back of the jalopy and came up with a length of rope. They hitched it to the back bumper of their car and tied the other end around the front bumper of the Bears' car.

"All aboard!" said Lem. And the Bogg brothers pulled away, towing the Bears' car behind them.

"Where are they taking us?" asked Mama.

Papa shrugged. "At least we're moving!"

Brother and Sister hoped that the Bogg brothers weren't taking them down to their old shack. They didn't want to meet that big pig.

They soon pulled into a run-down old filling station. Someone who looked like an older version of the Bogg brothers came out.

"Hello, Uncle Zeke," said Lem.

"Hello, Nephew," said Uncle Zeke. "What can I do you fer?"

"These poor folks broke down on the road," said Lem. "You reckon you can fix them up?"

"Let's take a look," said Uncle Zeke.

He looked under the car's hood.

"Radee-ator hose," he said. "Busted clean open. I should have another one of them around here somewheres."

Uncle Zeke rummaged around behind the filling station and soon came back with a radiator hose. He banged and clanged under the hood for a few more minutes.

"There," he said. "Good as new. We'll top off the radee-ator, and you folks can be on your way."

"Thank you very much!" said Papa, relieved. He shook hands with Uncle Zeke and the Bogg brothers.

"Thank you!" said Mama. "How much do we owe you?" asked Papa, reaching for his wallet.

"Nothin'," said Lem. "This one is on us. After all, we're neighbors."

"That's right," said Mama with a gulp. "We are. In fact, how would you neighbors like to come over to our house for dinner next week?"

Papa, Brother, and Sister all stared at Mama with their mouths open.

"That's right neighborly of you," said Lem. "Don't mind if we do! Shem's cookin' has been getting a bit tiresome—too much possum stew."

"We were on our way to the Bear Town Festival," said Papa. "Would you like to join us?"

"Sure would!" said Lem. "We ain't been to a big shindig since Grandpap's ninetieth birthday party!"

So, the Bear family drove to Bear Town with the Bogg brothers and Uncle Zeke.

They were a little late, but they hadn't missed much ... just Mayor Honeypot's welcoming speech. They all joined in the games, rides, and contests. When it was time for the fireworks, the Bogg brothers livened things up with some music of their own.

The next week, the Bogg brothers came over to the Bears' tree house for dinner. They wore their best clothes and got all spruced up for the occasion. They even brought a housewarming gift: a big pot of Shem's special possum stew.

It was delicious!

The Berenstain Bears
Faithful Friends

Lizzy Bruin was Sister Bear's very best friend. It seemed like they had been best friends for a very long time.

Sister was glad she had such a good friend. She could always rely on Lizzy to be there for her. They hardly ever fought or argued. Not, that is, until Sister started to spend more time with Suzy MacGrizzie.

Suzy was a new cub in town. At first, Sister and her friends didn't pay much attention to Suzy.

But then, Sister noticed how lonely Suzy was and invited her to play. From then on, Suzy was part of Sister's little group.

All of Sister's friends, including Lizzy, liked Suzy. She was one more cub to spend time with and enjoy.

But Suzy was a little different from the other cubs. For one thing, she read an awful lot. And she was interested in different things—science, for instance. Suzy invited Sister over one night to look at the sky.

"Wow!" said Sister, looking into the eyepiece at the moon. "It looks so close."

One day, Suzy asked Sister to go on a butterfly hunt with her. They took butterfly nets and went out into the fields.

Sister caught a big yellow butterfly with black stripes. Suzy caught one that had bright red and blue spots on it and long swallowtails. It was very beautiful. After they studied the butterflies for a while, they let them go, and the butterflies sailed up into the sky over the trees.

"They're so pretty!" said Sister.

On their way back, Suzy and Sister ran into Lizzy and their friends Anna and Millie. They were all carrying their Bearbie dolls.

"Hiya, gang!" called Sister. "Suzy and I were out catching butterflies. You should have seen the big yellow one I got!"

"Yeah, great," said Lizzy. "Well, see you, I guess."

"Wait a minute," said Sister. "Where are you all going?"

"We're going over to my garage to play Bearbie dolls," said Lizzy.

"Can Suzy and I come too?" asked Sister.

"It looks like you two are already pretty busy," said Lizzy.

"Come on, girls." With that, Lizzy and her friends went on their way.

"How do you like that?" said Sister, hurt and angry.

"Who does she think she is? Come on, Suzy, we'll play over at my house. Who needs them, anyway?"

When they got to the Bear family's tree house, Suzy and Sister found Brother Bear and Cousin Fred getting out their fishing tackle.

"Lizzy and your friends were here looking for you," Brother said. "I told them you were playing with Suzy. Lizzy didn't seem very happy."

"That Lizzy Bruin!" said Sister, annoyed. "What business is it of hers who I play with?"

"I guess she's jealous," said Brother.

"Jealous?" said Sister, puzzled.

"Sure," said Brother. "She's been your best friend for years. You mean a lot to her. She's just worried that maybe you don't like her as much as you used to."

"Oh," said Sister, "that's silly!" It was true that she liked her new friend, Suzy. But Lizzy would always be her best friend.

"What should I do?" Sister wondered out loud.

Cousin Fred spoke up. "You know what the Bible says: 'Wounds from a friend can be trusted.'" Fred liked to memorize things.

"Huh?" said both Sister and Brother. "What does that mean?"

Suzy answered—she liked to memorize things too. "I think it means that when a friend who loves you hurts your feelings, you need to find out what is bothering her."

"Yes," Fred nodded. "And the Bible also says that we shouldn't stay angry with our friends. God wants us to make up with them if we have an argument."

"Oh," said Sister, thoughtfully.

"I have an idea," said Brother. "Fred and I were about to go fishing. Why don't we grab some extra fishing gear and go over to Lizzy's? We can see if they would all like to go fishing with us."

"Great!" said Sister. Suzy grinned.

So they all stopped by Lizzy's garage on their way to the fishing hole.

"Hey, Lizzy!" called Sister. "Do you and Anna
and Millie want to go fishing with us?"

Lizzy acted like she wasn't so sure. But Anna
and Millie were all for it, and Lizzy certainly didn't
want to be left out.

Soon, they were all down at the
fishing hole. Lizzy cast her line out into
the middle of the pond and got her line
into a terrible tangle.

73

"Here, let me help you, Lizzy," said Sister, taking her fishing rod. "I'll untangle it for you."

"Wow, thanks!" said Lizzy. "You're a real friend, Sister."

"I always have been and I always will be!"
said Sister.
 And together they picked away at the
tangled fishing line.

The Berenstain Bears
THE
FORGIVING TREE

It was a special day in the tree house. It was Brother Bear's birthday.

"Happy birthday, Brother!" shouted the party guests as Mama brought in the cake. They all sang the birthday song.

"Make a wish!" said Sister. Brother closed his eyes, made a wish, and blew out the candles.

"YEA!" the guests yelled, clapping and blowing on noisemakers.

Papa cut the cake and everyone dug in.
"What did you wish for?" asked Cousin Fred.
"If I tell, it won't come true," said Brother.

When they were finished eating the cake, it was time to open presents. Brother got some very nice ones—a model plane, some books, a racing car set, and a video game.

Then, he noticed Papa sneaking into the next room. When he came back, Papa was pushing ... a brand-new bike!

"Wow!" said Brother excitedly. "It's exactly what I wished for!"

"Lucky you didn't tell Fred," said Sister.

"That's a beautiful bike," said Fred, admiring it. "I sure wish I had a bike like that."

"Oh," said Brother without thinking, "you can borrow it anytime you like."

"Gee, thanks!" said Fred.

"Let's try out your new video game," suggested Sister.

All the cubs crowded around while Brother and
Sister played the new video game. They were so
interested, they didn't notice anything else for a while.
But then Brother looked over at his brand-new bike. It
was gone!

"Hey!" said Brother. "Where's my new bike?"

"Say," said Lizzy, looking out the window, "isn't that Fred riding it?"

Lizzy was right. Cousin Fred was outside riding Brother's brand-new bike around the tree house. Brother was furious!

"That Fred!" growled Brother. "He can't do that!" And he charged outside.

"Uh-oh!" said Mama and Papa running after him.

But they were too late. Brother was already yelling for Fred to get off his bike. He startled him so much that poor Fred didn't look where he was going and ran right into the mailbox.

He wasn't hurt, but the bike was. The front wheel was bent and wouldn't turn.

"Look what you did!" shouted Brother. "Who said you could ride my new bike?"

"You did," said Fred. "You said I could borrow it anytime."

"I didn't mean right away," said Brother, stamping his feet. "I never even got to ride it!"

"Now Brother," said Mama, "calm down. This is just a misunderstanding. Fred didn't mean any harm."

"But my bike is ruined!" cried Brother. "Just look at it!"

"It's not ruined," said Papa. "We'll take it down to the bike shop and get it fixed up as good as new."

"But it won't be new!" said Brother. "It will never be brand-new again!" And he stormed off in a huff.

"Gee, I'm sorry," said Fred. He felt awful. "I never meant to hurt Brother or his new bike."

"Of course not, Fred," soothed Mama. "It was just an accident."

"I'm sorry Brother's so mad," said Fred. "Do you think he'll ever forgive me?"

"Of course he will," said Papa. "He'll get over it in no time."

But Sister wasn't so sure. She followed Brother to their backyard tree house.

"Mind if I come up?" she called. Brother didn't answer. Sister climbed the ladder and found Brother sitting, sulking, at the top.

"You're certainly in a good mood," said Sister.

"Humph!" grunted Brother.

Sister noticed a faded red line drawn down the middle of the tree house floor.

"Do you remember this red line?" she asked. Brother shrugged.

"We put it there a long time ago," Sister went on. "We were so mad at each other that we divided the tree house in half. I sat on one side, and you sat on the other. We sat out here being mad at each other until it started to rain and we got soaked. By that time we couldn't even remember what we were mad about."

"I guess so," said Brother.

As Brother and Sister sat in their tree house
it became cloudy and started to rain. They
went back to the party and found the guests
getting ready to break the piñata.

It was one Papa made in his workshop.
There were all kinds of candy inside but
especially licorice, since licorice was Papa's
favorite. Papa held the piñata out on a
broomstick.

"Okay," he said. "Start swinging. But be
careful not to hit me!"

One after another, the cubs whacked the piñata until it finally broke open, spilling candy onto the floor.

They all scrambled to grab some, including Papa. Brother scrambled right into Fred. In fact, they knocked heads.

"Ow!" said Fred rubbing his noggin.

"Oops, sorry!" said Brother.

"That's okay, Brother," said Fred. "I forgive you."

"I forgive you, too, Fred," said Brother, feeling ashamed of himself.

"I shouldn't have yelled at you about the bike before. It really was just an accident."

"Forget it," said Fred ... and forget it they did as they gathered up the candy.

"You know," said Papa to Mama as they watched the happy cubs, "that old tree in the backyard has seen a lot of forgiving over the years. I guess you'd call it a Forgiving Tree."

"As the Lord said," smiled Mama. "And forgive us our debts, as we forgive our debtors."

"What does that mean?" asked Sister.

"Just that God wants us to forgive those who hurt our feelings," said Mama.

"And, remember," added Papa, "though God wants us to be good, he forgives us when we do something wrong."

"Well, I think that's very nice of God," said Sister.

"Yes," agreed Mama and Papa, "it is!"

The Berenstain Bears
AND THE
BIGGEST BRAG

Brother and Sister Bear were
talented young cubs. They were good
at all sorts of things, and they worked
hard at the things they were good at.
They studied hard at school.
They practiced hard at sports.

They put a lot of time and effort into art and music. They even put a lot of brainpower into playing games.

Brother and Sister were proud of their talents. They were proud of all their hard work and effort.

As a matter of fact, Brother and Sister were so proud of their talents that they sometimes bragged about them. They bragged about them mostly to each other. And it seemed to Mama and Papa they were always trying to top one another.

"I got an A in math," Brother bragged to Sister.

"Well, smarty," Sister bragged back, "I got an A+!"

"I scored a goal in my soccer game," Sister bragged to Brother.

"Oh, yeah?" Brother bragged back. "I scored the winning goal in my game and set up another goal with a corner kick!"

"Really!" said Mama. "Can't you two stop your endless bragging and boasting? You're both very talented cubs. Why do you have to top each other?"

"Besides," said Papa. "It's not a loving thing for a brother and sister to do. You know what the Bible says about love—'It does not envy, it does not boast, it is not proud.'"

But Brother and Sister still felt they had to be the best at everything, and they went right on with their bragging, boasting ways.

One day, after school, Brother and Sister were taking a well-deserved rest from all their hard work. They stopped at the top of a hill on their way home and lay in the soft grass looking up at the puffy white clouds. Brother and Sister imagined they saw shapes in the clouds.

"You know," said Sister, "that cloud up there looks like a big fluffy sheep."

It did, indeed, look like a fleecy white sheep grazing in a great blue meadow.

"Well," said Brother, "I think that cloud over there looks like a galloping white horse."

Sister had to admit it looked a lot like a horse. Brother's galloping white horse seemed more interesting than her fleecy white sheep. So she looked around for something better.

"I think that cloud over there looks like a dragon breathing fire and smoke," she said.

"Hmm!" said Brother. At first he didn't see it. But the more he looked, the more it did look like a dragon. He was a little annoyed. Seeing a fire-breathing dragon in a cloud was a lot better than a galloping white horse.

"Oh, yeah?" he said. "Well I think the cloud next to it looks like a knight in armor fighting the dragon." He thought some more. "And behind him there's a castle on a hill with a fair maiden who the dragon was going to eat but the knight is rescuing her." And he said to himself, So there!

Sister stared at the clouds, grumpily. She was not pleased that Brother had topped her dragon. Then she had an idea.

"I think those clouds look like a fleet of pirate ships shooting their cannons at a tropical island with a big fort. There's a little town with houses and church towers and swaying palm trees filled with monkeys," Sister said, and added to herself, Top that!

Brother was upset. How could he top a whole fleet of pirate ships and an island with swaying palm trees and monkeys? He stared at the sky, sulking. But then he noticed something.

"You know," he said, holding his hands up to the sky and looking through them, "if you look at these clouds just right ..." he squinted at them,

" … they look like the whole Solar System. The sun is in the center, then Mercury, Venus, the Earth with the moon, Mars, asteroids, Jupiter, Saturn, Neptune, Uranus, and the Kuiper Belt with Pluto, and …"

"Oh, yeah?" shouted Sister who was mad because she had no idea what the Kuiper Belt was. "I don't think they look like the whole Solar System at all. And besides …!"

"Woah! Woah!" said a voice. "Hold your horses, up here. What's all the fussing and fretting about?"

It was Grizzly Gramps strolling by. He was out for a walk on this lovely afternoon, looking up at the puffy white clouds just like Brother and Sister.

Sister and Brother angrily explained about their "topping" contest.

"And Brother is cheating," complained Sister. "He doesn't really see any belt up there. He's just showing off!"

"Well, let me see," said Grizzly Gramps. "I'll bet I can see things up in those clouds too." He gazed up at the clouds, rubbing his chin.

"You know," he said, "I think I see two faces in the clouds."

"Where?" said the cubs.

"Right there," said Gramps. "They look like the faces of two of the biggest, bragging-est fools I ever saw."

"Who?" asked the cubs eagerly.

"You two!" said Gramps. "None other than Brother and Sister Bear!"

"But, Gramps!" protested Brother and Sister.

"Don't 'But, Gramps!' me," said Gramps. "Admit it! Don't you two feel foolish? All this bragging and boasting about something as silly as who can see what in a cloud?"

Now that they thought about it, it did seem sort of silly. What exactly were they bragging about?

"Remember what the Bible says," Gramps told them. "'Where there is strife, there is pride.'"

"We'll remember, Gramps," said the cubs.

"Now, you two come on over to my house," said Gramps. "Gran will give you milk and cookies, and we'll have a nice game of checkers."

"Okay, Gramps!" said the cubs.

"I bet I win at checkers," said Brother.

"No, I'm going to win," said Sister.

"Cubs!" said Gramps.

"Oops, sorry!" said the cubs, remembering not to brag.

111

The Berenstain Bears
AND THE GIFT OF COURAGE

112

Sister loved all animals—not only dogs and cats and birds and bunnies, but lizards and frogs and worms and bugs as well. She knew they were all God's creatures, and she liked to play with them. That's what caused the trouble with Too-Tall.

Too-Tall Grizzly and his gang were the official bullies of Bear Country School. They thought it was fun to push other cubs around, and they had many nasty ways to have fun.

One of their favorites was to bump into a cub on purpose and then make him apologize for being so clumsy.

Of course, they teased anyone anytime about pretty much anything at all. That's what happened to Sister Bear one morning in the schoolyard.

Sister was standing in line, waiting for the school
bell to ring, when a cute little ladybug landed right on
her shoulder.

She held out her finger so the ladybug could crawl onto it, and she chanted a line from an old nursery rhyme.

"Ladybug, ladybug, fly away home!"

As she watched the ladybug whirr away, Sister heard a nasty voice behind her. It was Too-Tall Grizzly.

"Ladybug, ladybug!" mocked Too-Tall. "Does Sister Bear wuv her wittle wadybug fwends?" he said in a silly, baby-talk voice. The rest of his gang laughed, and quite a few other cubs standing in line laughed with them.

Sister felt so embarrassed she froze. She didn't know what to say or do. She just stood there. Then the school bell rang, and the line began to move. She never got a chance to say or do anything at all.

For the rest of the day, Sister Bear felt terrible. She wished she had stood up against that nasty Too-Tall. She kept thinking of things that she "should have" said. Maybe, she thought, I was just plain scared! She didn't like the idea of being scared.

By bedtime that evening, Sister had almost stopped worrying about the Too-Tall incident—almost. It was Papa Bear's turn to read a bedtime story.

"What will it be tonight?" asked Papa as Brother and Sister snuggled down in their bunk beds.

A thought came into Sister's head. "How about David and Goliath?" she suggested.

"Yes," agreed Brother, "that's a good story."

"All right," said Papa. He got the *Big Book of Bible Stories* down from the bookshelf and settled in to read.

"Long ago in the Holy Land, there lived a young shepherd named David. It was his job to watch over his father's flock of sheep. He knew that God was with him, so he was not afraid of wolves or lions.

"When wolves came sneaking up to the flock, David drove them away with stones from his sling.

"In those days, there was a giant warrior named Goliath who towered over all other warriors. No one was brave enough to fight him.

"David heard about Goliath, but David was not afraid. He knew God was watching over him. So he took some stones and his sling and went out against Goliath.

"When Goliath saw David, he laughed because David was only a boy. He raised his great spear to throw it at David.

"But David quickly put a stone in his sling and swung it around and around his head. He let it fly, and it struck Goliath right on his forehead. Goliath fell with a crash that shook the earth.

"Little David had struck down the giant warrior! With God's help, David had shown great courage and saved the land."

The story was done. "David was very brave, wasn't he?" asked Brother as Papa kissed them good night.

"He had the bravest heart of all," nodded Papa. "You know what they say, 'Little David was small—but, oh, my!'"

"I don't think I'm brave enough to stand up to someone so much bigger than I am," said Sister. "I would probably be too scared to even move."

"I don't know about that," said Papa. "I think both of you can be quite brave when you need to be. And remember, God is watching over you just like David. That will give you courage."

The next morning, Brother and Sister set off for school bright and early. As they strolled along the road, they heard laughing and shouting up ahead. They rounded a bend and saw Too-Tall Grizzly and his gang.

"I wonder what they're up to," said Brother.

"No good, I'll bet," said Sister.

As they came closer, they saw that the gang was throwing rocks up into a tree.

"What's going on, Too-Tall?" asked Brother.

"You're just in time for some fun!" Too-Tall laughed. "See that hornets' nest up there?" He pointed at a huge round nest hanging high in the tree. "We're going to knock it down and see what happens."

"Don't do that!" said Sister. "That nest is the hornets' home. If you knock it down, they'll have no place to live."

"Aaaw!" sneered Too-Tall. "Are those hornets more of your wittle buggy fwends? Why don't you 'fly away' and mind your own business?"

While the gang laughed, Too-Tall drew back his arm to hurl a big rock at the nest. But Sister grabbed onto his arm.

"Hey, you little squirt!" yelled Too-Tall. "Let go!"

The rest of the gang charged at Sister to pull her away, but Brother stepped right in front of them. He glared at them. They didn't like the look in his eyes. He didn't seem the least bit afraid. They all backed away.

Too-Tall swung Sister around and around like David with his sling. But Sister hung on for all she was worth. Finally, Too-Tall gave a great heave and broke Sister's grip.

The rock flew out of his hand and sailed up into the tree. It smacked right into the hornets' nest and knocked it open. A big cloud of angry hornets flew out.

Brother and Sister ducked under some bushes. The hornets bunched themselves up into an angry black ball and headed down after Too-Tall and his gang.

"Yeow!" yelled Too-Tall. "Look out!"

"Run!" yelled the gang.

When they were gone, Brother and Sister peeked out from behind the tree. "That was close!" said Brother.

"Do you think God was watching over us?" wondered Sister.

"No doubt about it!" nodded Brother. With a sigh of relief, they continued on their way to school.

"You were very brave," said Brother, "going after Too-Tall that way. 'Little Sister was small—but, *oh my!*'"

Sister laughed. "You were pretty brave yourself, standing up to the whole gang that way."

"I guess Papa was right," said Brother. "Even young cubs like us can be brave when we need to be."

"Too-Tall wasn't very brave," said Sister.

"Let's be fair," said Brother. "No one is very brave when it comes to angry hornets."

"No doubt about it!" agreed Sister, and they walked on to school arm in arm.

The Berenstain Bears
Blessed are the Peacemakers

The Bear Country School was mostly a peaceful sort of place. Most of the cubs got along with each other most of the time. True, there could be minor squabbles.

Voices were sometimes raised.

Angry words were sometimes spoken.

But most of the time, most of the cubs were calm and peaceful—except for Too-Tall Grizzly and his gang.

Too-Tall's gang had the most trouble with Ferdy Factual and his friends. Ferdy was one of the best students in the school. His friends were cubs like Cousin Fred and Trudy Brunowitz who were good students just like him. Too-Tall's gang and Ferdy's friends simply did not get along.

Brother and Sister Bear did not belong to either group. They liked to get along with everyone, including Too-Tall and Ferdy, and they did.

But one thing that everyone at the school did agree on was the All-School Play. It was the biggest event of the year. Anyone could try out for a part and everyone helped with scenery, sets, and other jobs. All the students' families came to the performance as well as other folks from around Bear Country who just enjoyed a good show.

This year's play was *Romeo and Grizzliet*. Students crowded into the auditorium for tryouts.

All the cubs tried out for parts one after the other.

Finally, Teacher Jane announced the roles. Brother and Sister had small parts. Even Too-Tall had a role.

But the main roles, Romeo and Grizzliet, went to
Ferdy Factual and Queenie McBear. Everyone was a little
surprised. After all, Queenie was part of Too-Tall's gang
and usually she and Ferdy did not get along. Things could
get a little weird with them playing a boy and girl who were
... *in love!*

After tryouts, Too-Tall decided
to make trouble with Ferdy.
"Look out!" said Too-Tall,
bumping into Ferdy on purpose.

"Hey! Watch where you're going!" said Ferdy.
"You wanna make something of it?" asked Too-Tall.
Ferdy's friend, Trudy Brunowitz, came up.
"Yes," she said. "We do!"
"You leave Too-Tall alone!" said Queenie
coming up to help Too-Tall.
Too-Tall's gang and Ferdy's friends gathered
around. Brother and Sister saw what
was happening and rushed over.
They didn't want any of their friends
to get hurt.

"Okay, okay! Break it up!" said Brother, getting in between Too-Tall and Ferdy. Sister got between Queenie and Trudy.

"Let's remember what it says in the Bible," said Cousin Fred. "'Peacemakers who sow in peace reap a harvest of righteousness.'"

"What's that supposed to mean?" said Too-Tall.

"It means if you make peace," explained Ferdy, "you will get a rich reward."

"Oh, cool," said Too-Tall. "Well … you just stay away from Queenie, except in the school play—and not too close there either, pal."

"Really, Too-Tall!" said Queenie. "I can take care of myself."

The Story of Romeo & Grizzliet

There were rehearsals for the school play every day. Romeo and Grizzliet was quite an exciting story. It was about two families who did not get along at all. But when a boy and a girl from each family fell in love and wanted to get married, the two families became even angrier.

A big fight broke out with sword fighting and everything!

Soon, the night of the big play arrived. Families of all the cubs in school came and lots of other folks from all around Bear Country too. Mayor and Mrs. Honeypot were there, as well as Preacher Brown and his wife. Even Squire and Lady Grizzly decided to come.

The play was going beautifully. In the middle, Romeo and Grizzliet stood on a balcony to say how much they loved each other. It was very convincing. In fact, it was a little too convincing for Too-Tall.

"Hey, you little fur ball!" he suddenly yelled. "You leave Queenie alone!"

Too-Tall started to climb up onto the balcony to get at Ferdy.

When Too-Tall's gang and Ferdy's friends who were in the play saw what was happening, they got upset. They started to push and shove. They started to yell and shout.

When the families in the audience saw their cubs fighting on stage, they got angry too. They started heading for the stage to help their cubs. Everybody was getting into the act!

"STOP!" cried a very loud voice. It was Squire Grizzly. He was quickly up on stage with Mayor Honeypot and Preacher Brown. They stood in the middle of the crowd and held them apart.

"Stop this disgraceful brawling at once!" said Squire Grizzly. "You should all be ashamed of yourselves!"

"But," began Too-Tall, "it all started with this little fuzz face …"

"I don't want to hear any name-calling, and there'll be no excuses," interrupted the Squire. "There's never an excuse for starting a fight."

"That's right," said Preacher Brown. "Remember what the Bible says, 'Turn from evil and do good; seek peace and pursue it.'"

Everyone felt ashamed and very foolish. Brother and Sister, who had rushed forward to help with the peacekeeping on stage, now helped the audience back to their seats, and the play went on.

It was a great success. At the end, the cast lined up on the stage. All the cubs—Too-Tall's gang and Ferdy's friends included—joined hands and bowed. The applause was loud and long.

After the great Romeo and Grizzliet fight, things were different between Too-Tall's gang and Ferdy's friends. They never exactly became best buds. But now there was peace between them. And the peace-loving peacemakers, Brother and Sister Bear, were good friends to them all as usual.

The Berenstain Bears

Get Involved

Brother and Sister Bear belonged to the Cub Club at the Chapel in the Woods. Preacher Brown was their leader. They did lots of fun things together. They went on picnics, played baseball, sang in the chorus, put on plays, and painted pictures of Bible stories. But the Cub Club was about much more than just doing fun things.

The real purpose of the club was to help others. There was always something that needed to be done around Bear Country. Sometimes it was cleaning up the Beartown playground. Sometimes it was bringing food to bears who couldn't get out and about. Sometimes it was even fixing up old houses for folks who couldn't fix them up themselves.

Brother and Sister liked to be helpful. It made them feel good deep down inside. Preacher Brown explained that it was always a good thing to help those in need.

"As the Bible says," he told them, "'Whoever is kind to the needy honors God.'"

So the Cub Club went right on helping others all over Bear Country.

Little did they know that very soon their help would be truly needed indeed!

On the way to school one day, Brother and Sister noticed the sky growing very dark.

By the time they reached school, it was starting to drizzle.

Through the morning, it rained harder and harder. It rained so hard that recess was cancelled, and they had a study period instead.

"Rain, rain, go away," recited Sister. "Come again some other day."

But the rain paid no attention. It came pouring down harder than ever.

"I think you made it worse," said Brother.

When school let out, the cubs splashed their way home through the puddles. But then they heard a car coming down the road. It was Mama. She was coming to pick them up.

"Thanks, Mama," said the cubs. "We were getting soaked!"

At bedtime, Brother and Sister could hear the wind howling and the rain beating against the windows. It was a little spooky, but they snuggled down under the covers and soon drifted off to sleep. They dreamed about rushing streams and roaring waterfalls.

It was still raining when they woke up next morning.

"Wow!" said Brother. "Look at it coming down!"

As Brother and Sister went downstairs, they heard Papa on the phone.

"Don't worry," he said. "I'll be right over!"

"Over where?" asked Mama.

"That was Preacher Brown," said Papa. "The river is rising fast, and we'll need to get everyone out of their houses down there. We're meeting at the chapel."

"We'll all come with you," said Mama. "There'll be plenty for everyone to do."

At the Chapel in the Woods, bears were gathering from all over. Their cars were loaded with shovels and buckets, bundles of blankets, and boxes of food. Grizzly Gus had a load of sandbags in his truck.

Preacher Brown saw Brother, Sister, and some of the other cubs. "I want all you Cub Club members to go along with your dads and help out," he told them. "This is what the Cub Club is all about!"

"Yes, sir!" they said. They were glad to be going. And Brother and Sister especially wanted to make sure Cousin Fred was all right.

The cars drove through the storm, down to the river.

"We're just in time," said Papa. "The water is nearly up to the houses."

An angry river was swirling over its banks and lapping toward the houses.

"Look! There's Cousin Fred!" said Sister.

Cousin Fred, with Uncle Willie and Aunt Min, was leaning out of an upstairs window and waving.

The bears all set to work piling up sandbags and digging ditches to keep the water away from the houses. Brother, Sister, Cousin Fred, and the rest of the Cub Club joined in. They dug and dug and dug until they were cold, wet, and tired.

Then everyone drove back to the chapel to warm up, dry off, and get something to eat.

Preacher Brown got up in the pulpit, opened the Bible, and started to read: "The floodgates of the heavens were opened. And rain fell on the earth ... The waters flooded the earth ..."

Sister noticed a bright light coming through the chapel windows.

"Look!" she said. "The rain is stopping, and the sun is coming out!"

"And there's a rainbow!" said Brother.

"I have set my rainbow in the clouds ...," read Preacher Brown, closing the Bible.

"With God's help, we are all safe and sound," said Preacher Brown. "Thanks to everyone for pitching in and helping out."

All the bears clapped. They had been there to help others when their help was truly needed.

The Berenstain Bears' Gossip Gang

Lizzy and Suzy were Sister Bear's best friends. They liked doing all sorts of things together. They rode bikes and jumped rope. Sometimes they just sat around and talked. They talked about TV shows and toys, about games and songs, about pets, parents, brothers and sisters and, of course, their other friends.

"Did you get a load of that new cub in school?" asked Suzy. "His name is actually Teddy Bear!" The others laughed. Suzy had been a new cub not so long ago. But she didn't seem to remember.

"Well, I saw Anna Bruin the other day," said Sister, "and, you know, I think she put on some weight. She looks sort of chubby."

Lizzy and Suzy giggled.

The three friends talked for a while longer but it was soon dinnertime.

"See you!" said Sister, heading home. She liked talking to Lizzy and Suzy about other cubs. It made her feel special and "in-the-know."

Back home, Mama and Papa were setting the table. Brother and Sister joined them.

"Do you know what Herb the mailman told me?" Papa said to Mama as he laid the silverware.

"I can't imagine," said Mama, busy putting out plates.

"He said someone saw Mayor Honeypot throwing a banana peel out his car window. Imagine—the mayor, himself, a litterbug!"

"Now, Papa," said Mama. "You know that's just gossip. You shouldn't spread stories like that."

Papa looked a little ashamed. "I guess you're right. It was just so interesting."

As they sat down to dinner, Sister had a question.

"Mama," she asked, "what's gossip?"

"Well," Mama began, "gossip is when we tell stories about others—especially stories that make them look bad. It's something we do to make ourselves feel special. It can be very hurtful. As the Bible says, 'gossip separates close friends.'"

"Oh," said Sister, worried. She thought maybe saying that Anna looked sort of chubby was gossip. She decided not to think about it anymore.

The next day, Sister saw Lizzy and Suzy walking ahead of her on the way to the playground. They were busy talking and didn't notice Sister coming up behind them. As Sister drew near, she overheard them talking ... about her!

"Do you know what Anna told me about Sister?" began Lizzy.

"No, what?" asked Suzy, eagerly.

"She saw Sister's spelling quiz when Teacher Jane was handing back the papers, and it was marked, '60%—very poor!'" said Lizzy.

When Sister heard that, she stopped short. In the first place, it wasn't true. Her quiz was marked "70%—fair."

And, in the second place, why were Lizzy and Suzy gossiping about her?

They were supposed to be her best friends. She felt so bad she hid behind a tree until Lizzy and Suzy were out of sight.

As Sister came out from behind the tree, Brother Bear walked by. He was on his way to play catch with Cousin Fred.

"Why are you hiding behind a tree?" he said.

"I didn't want Lizzy and Suzy to see me," said Sister.

"Why not?" he asked.

"Because they were gossiping about me and I heard," said Sister. "I was so embarrassed!"

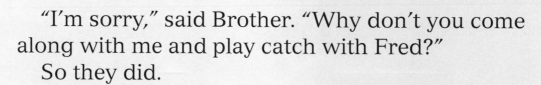

"I'm sorry," said Brother. "Why don't you come along with me and play catch with Fred?"

So they did.

At the playground, they started tossing the ball around. Sister could see Lizzy and Suzy on the swings, nearby. They waved and Sister waved back. Then she got angry.

"You know what I heard about Lizzy?' she called, loudly, to Fred. "I heard that she is a big silly dope!"

"Huh?" said Fred.

"And you know what I heard about Suzy?" she yelled, even louder. "I heard that she is a funny-faced noodle-brain!"

"Sister!" said Brother.

When Lizzy and Suzy overheard Sister, they jumped off the swings and came charging over.

"Why are you saying bad things about us?" they yelled. "We thought you were our best friend!"

"That's just what I thought!" said Sister. "But I heard you gossiping about me on the way here!"

"Oh," said Lizzy. She hadn't thought about it that way. "I guess you're right. We were gossiping about you. I'm sorry!"

"Me, too!" said Suzy.

Sister got over being angry right away. After all, Lizzy and Suzy were her best friends.

"That's okay," she said. "Maybe it would be better if we just didn't gossip about anyone."

"As it says in the Bible," said Fred, "'The tongue also is a fire.'"

"What's that supposed to mean?" said Sister.

"Just that gossiping is like playing with fire," said Fred. "You can get burned."

"A game of baseball would be more fun than gossip," suggested Brother.

"Yes," added Sister. "Let's play ball!"

And they did.

GOD BLESS OUR HOME

The Bear family, who lived down a sunny dirt road deep in Bear Country, loved their tree house home. They lived inside a great hollow, old oak tree. They moved there when Brother Bear was little, from a cave way up in the mountains. That was before Honey or Sister Bear were even born.

All in all, the tree house was a fine place to live. The thick wood of the tree trunk kept them warm in the winter. The spreading oak leaves above kept the house shady and cool in the summer.

Brother and Sister loved to lie in bed in the evening and fall asleep to the sound of crickets and katydids in the branches outside.

In the morning, they woke to the sound of a mockingbird singing his copycat song at their open window.

The Bear family was very happy in their tree house. It's true, it was a little small. And when baby Honey came along, it suddenly seemed even smaller.

At first, Mama and Papa just put Honey's crib in their room alongside their bed. That was okay. While she was very small, Honey needed to be near them anyway.

But when Honey started to grow, it wasn't so fine. She started climbing out of her crib and crawling into bed with Mama and Papa. She would sleep between them sideways and kick them in the stomach. Mama and Papa weren't getting enough sleep.

One morning, at breakfast, a sleepy Papa said to a sleepy Mama, "You know, maybe it's time we thought about moving to a bigger house."

"Mmm!" said Mama, half asleep. "Maybe you're right."

But Brother and Sister overheard them.

"Move to a bigger house!" they both said. "No way! We love our tree house!"

"We love it too," said Mama. "But I'm afraid it's getting too small for our growing family. Honey really needs a room of her own."

"And there's no garage for our car," added Papa. "I have been parking in the drive for years now, since my workshop is in the garage. When it snows, I have to shovel it out every time."

"But there must be a way to make more room and keep living right here," said Brother.

"Yes," agreed Sister. "We just need to put on our thinking caps."

So the family took a tour of the tree house, inside and out, looking into every room, poking into every nook, and peering into every cranny.

Papa got out his tape measure and made some notes.

"I think I know what to do," said Papa. "I can enlarge the basement, move some things down from the attic, and divide off part of the attic into a room for Honey."

"That would work nicely," said Mama. "What about the car?"

"Simple," said Papa. "I'll just build a shed onto the side of the garage. That will keep the car out of the snow."

The next day, with the cubs' help, Papa set to work. After many days of hard work, it was all finished.

"You know," said Papa, as he looked over their brand-new old home, "this isn't a bad little place, at that."

"Not bad?" said the cubs. "It's the best little place in the whole wide world!"

"Yes," said Mama, "and above all, it is our own home, sweet home." She pointed to the sampler on the wall. "May God always bless our happy home."

The Berenstain Bears®
Here's the Church, Here's the Steeple

The Bear family is going to the Chapel in the Woods. Mama and Papa go first.

"Come along, Brother, Sister, and Honey."

"Here's the church and here's the steeple," Sister Bear said. "Open the doors, and see all the people!"

Inside the chapel, everyone sits down. The Widder Bruin plays the organ, and everyone takes out their hymn books to sing.

Soon Preacher Brown walks into the chapel. Everyone opens their Bibles to read.

Preacher Brown goes to the pulpit and says,
"Let us praise the Lord for this day."

The cubs stay for awhile but then it is time to go to Sunday school.

In Sunday school, the cubs draw pictures of Bible stories.

They put on costumes and perform a Bible play.
It is the story of Daniel in the lions' den.

Sunday school is over, and the cubs join their parents. Services are over too.

All the bears get ready to head home.

"Open the doors," Sister Bear sings, "and see all the people."